Tales in Rhyme

Cinderella

Sia Gupta

Om KIDZ
An imprint of Om Books International

Cinderella

I will tell you a tale in rhyme,
That once upon a time,
In a mansion was born a girl,
Beautiful like a shimmering pearl!

Her name was Ella,
She was a lovely bella.
She had a sweet and kind mother,
Like her, you wouldn't find another.

But Ella's mother got sick and died.
And while her father really tried
To take care of her all alone,
It made him tired to the bone.

He had to travel for work;
His duties he could not shirk.
So he married a widowed lady
Who turned out to be very shady.

She had two young daughters
Who looked like ugly little otters.
Ella's father needed to leave home
For work, far and wide he would roam.

As soon as Ella's father went away,
All the evil stepmother had to say,
'My word! This house is a mess.
Ella, make it fit for a princess.'

She soon took over the entire house,
And screamed at Ella on seeing a mouse.
She would lock Ella in the dingy attic;
Oh God! It was so very tragic.

Ella did all the household chores and duties,
While the daughters preened themselves as beauties.
Ella was having a depressing and hard time,
Her stepmother didn't even give her a dime!

And then one dreary, miserable day,
A man in a carriage came to say,
'Your father, my dear, has passed away,
My condolences on this very sad day. '

When Ella's stepmother heard,
She danced about like a happy bird;
She sang, 'Now I will have my say,'
And shouted 'Hip-hip hurray!'

'For this grand house is finally mine,
My authority here, will make it shine.
This big house is all for me,'
All three, then danced with glee.

After that day, Ella was treated like a maid;
Of her stepsisters, she was afraid.
She couldn't even sleep at night,
Oh! When would everything be alright?

And because she cleaned the fireplace,
There were cinders on her arms and face.
The stepsisters renamed Ella,
And started calling her Cinderella!

Prince Charming lived in that kingdom,
Everyone knew he was very handsome.
The prince was now ready to marry,
The family tradition he had to carry.

He had a dream of an ideal girl in mind,
Who was beautiful, intelligent and kind.
He decided to have a royal ball;
The ladies were invited, one and all.

The king was looking forward to the ball;
He had dreams which were grand and tall.
He wanted a grandchild he would enjoy,
He could not wait for his son to give him that joy!

So the letters were sent far and away,
They arrived everywhere, night and day.
When the stepmother read her invite,
She exclaimed with utmost delight!

She wanted her own daughter to be the queen,
In her mind, the picture could be clearly seen.
The stepsisters had high hopes too,
They wanted to do the best they could do.

All the girls must also mean me,
Wondered Cinderella, happily.
'Oh! Can I also go please?'
She asked, bending on her knees.

The stepsisters shouted, 'No, No!'
They really didn't want Ella to go.
The stepmother said, 'I will decide.
Both of you please go inside.'

'Ella, I will only allow you to go,
If your dress is as pretty as a bow.
And make sure your chores are all done,
Otherwise you will miss all the fun.'

Cinderella said, 'Oh! thank you,
I am looking forward to it too.'
Her little mice friends got to know;
They decided to put on a show.

'Let's make a dress for Cinderella,
And make her look like a royal bella!'
They crept into the stepsisters room,
Which was filled with an eerie gloom.

Borrowing a necklace and a sash
That the stepsisters thought was trash,
The mice made her a beautiful dress,
Which was truly fit for a princess.

When Ella wore it and went downstairs,
The stepsisters gave her jealous stares.
'That's our sash and necklace,' they cried,
And tore Ella's dress from the side.

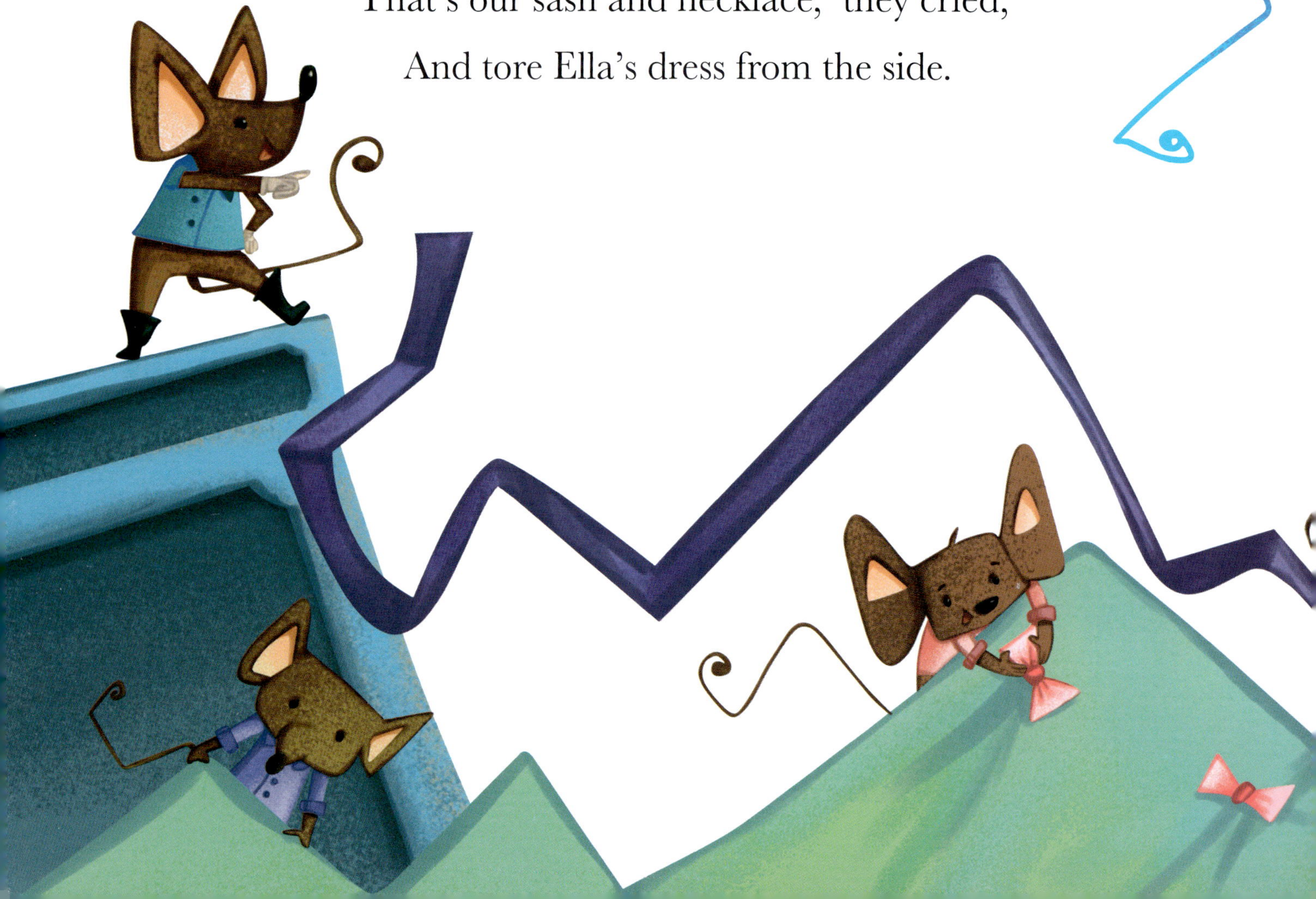

'We will have to leave you behind,'
Said the stepmother, unjust and unkind.
They went, leaving Ella heartbroken outside,
Where she cried, and cried, and cried.

At that very same moment,
Ella heard some movement.
She saw a woman with a bag,
Who looked like a dirty, old hag.

She asked for some water and food;
Ella being kind, brightened up her mood.
She got the lady something to eat and drink,
And suddenly the lady began to shrink.

Then she, to her original size grew back.
This time, not wearing a horrendous sack.
She looked like an angelic fairy,
Not even a tiny bit scary!

‘Who are you?’ Cinderella exclaimed.
The pretty lady, then explained,
‘I am your one and only fairy godmother.
Didn’t you hear about me from your mother?’

‘Now why do you look sad, dear?
Is there something you fear?’
‘No, I just want to go to the ball,
To dance with a prince in the grand hall.’

'Why have you been crying then?
You look like a frail, dying hen.
Come, let's get you a carriage and dress;
Some important guests we have to impress!'

Then she said in a clear voice,
'Don't worry, you will truly rejoice.
Now first I need a squishy fruit;
A watermelon, I think will suit.'

'But I don't have a watermelon;
Not even a small, yellow lemon!
I have some pumpkins for you.
Should I get you one or two?'

First, she got the biggest one.
The godmother said, 'Well done!'
And then she whispered some spells,
Making a carriage decorated with bells.

Then she turned the mice to horses,
Using all her majestic magical forces.
They were strong and beautiful.
She made sure they were dutiful.

She turned the horse into a coachman,
While the dog was turned into a footman.
She led Cinderella to her golden carriage,
To be the bride in a possible, royal marriage.

'But I can't go like this!' Cinderella said,
'I don't even look pretty from toe to head.'
Quickly the godmother made her a gown,
One that was fit for a lady with a crown.

Then she made the shiny, glass slipper,
And said something in a low whisper.
'You must definitely be back at midnight,
Or you will be in for a terrible fright.'

'Your carriage, horses and uniformed men,
Will come back to normal, young woman!'
'I will remember it,' Cinderella vowed.
'I will try my best to make you proud.'

'Well, go and enjoy yourself a lot;
And just give it your very best shot,'
Said the godmother, wishing her well,
And then she disappeared with a spell.

In her carriage, Cinderella rushed to the ball;
It looked magnificent beyond recall.
She got out and climbed up the stairs,
The people gave her smiles, sighs and stares.

She went inside and looked around,
And soon she heard a musical sound.
So she went to the hall and saw the prince,
In boredom he stood, hard to convince.

He saw Cinderella, his dreams came true.
He forgot that he had been feeling blue.
'Would you do me the honour of a dance?'
Asked the prince, waiting for his chance.

'Of course, Sire, I will,' Cinderella said,
And then the prince bowed his head.
The king watched, squealing with joy,
Already imagining a baby girl or boy!

He told his advisor, 'Fall in love, they must,
For this job, you are the only one I trust.'
The prince and Ella had a lovely time,
Chattering while they drank water with lime.

Then suddenly the clock struck midnight,
Which gave Cinderella a big fright.
She worried that the spell would fade,
So long she should not have stayed.

As she ran down the magnificent stairs,
Parting the crowd of jealous ladies with airs,
Suddenly her dainty glass slipper fell out,
Which Cinderella had to make do without.

She kept running and could not wait,
For she had to be out of the palace gate.
The bewildered prince tried to follow her,
But he only found her glass slipper.

At home, Cinderella was sweeping the floors,
As well as polishing the windows and doors.
And while she was thinking about her dance,
The prince was thinking about their brief romance.

Cinderella hid her glass slipper in a box,
Where she kept her shoes and socks.
When the stepsisters reached home,
They sat quietly below the parlour dome.

They cried that it was so unfair!
'We are both so beautiful and fair.'
The stepmother was also sad,
Oh! The dreams she had had!

Soon, the king's messenger came to ask,
As they had a very important task;
Carrying the glass slipper on a tray,
The kings men had this to say.

'For the young and beautiful girl,
Who the prince had spun in a twirl.
The girl who wears this shoe,
Will be the one to go through.'

'She will be the true princess,
The only one the king will bless.
This young lady we have to find,
Or the prince will go out of his mind!'

The messengers were on a quest;
They said, 'We have a simple request.
Your daughters must try this glass shoe,
Is there any other pretty lady here too?'

'Just us,' said the first stepsister, as she tried;
When the shoe didn't fit, she howled and cried.
Then the second daughter also tried to put
The shiny glass slipper on to her big foot.

When the slipper did not at all fit,
She almost had a humongous fit.
Just then, Cinderella came down;
The stepmother gave her a frown.

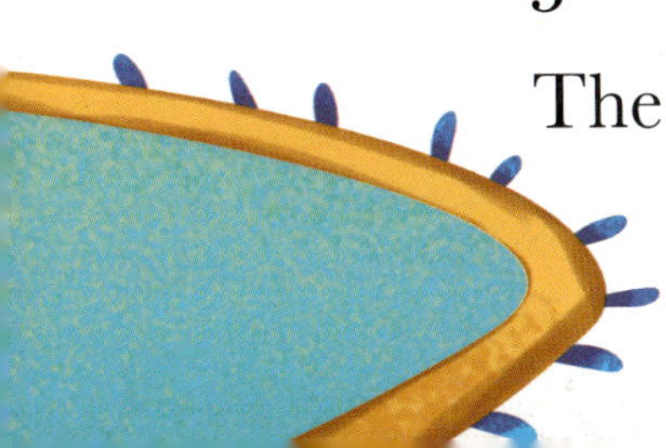

‘May I also try it?’ she meekly said.
But the stepmother said, ‘Go to bed.’
Then the advisor gave out a cry
That every young lady must try.

The stepmother broke the slipper with a crash.
‘Sorry!’ she said and threw it in the trash.
‘Oh no!’ the advisor in distress, shouted,
The intentions of this lady, he now doubted.

Cinderella told him not to worry;
She left the room in a terrible hurry.
She came back with a matching shoe,
And the advisor said, 'Thank you!'

The glass slipper fit Cinderella so well,
This was definitely the girl, he could tell.
He took her to the palace as his guest,
He was happy to complete his quest.

The king was informed straight away;
He was waiting for this lovely day.
For their wedding he planned a grand affair,
One that all the kingdom would gleefully share.

Ella and the prince were so in love,
As the fairy godmother watched from above!
Ella and the prince married in joy and laughter,
And they lived happily ever after!